Oliver Moon and the Monster Mystery

Sue Mongredien

Illustrated by

Jan McCafferty

USBORNE

For Ben Smailes
with lots of love

First published in 2009 by Usborne Publishing Ltd., Usborne House,
83-85 Saffron Hill, London EC1N 8RT, England. www.usborne.com

Text copyright © Sue Mongredien Ltd., 2009

Illustration copyright © Usborne Publishing Ltd., 2009

A CIP catalogue record for this book is available from
the British Library.

UK ISBN 9780746090756 First published in America in 2011 AE.

American ISBN 9780794530952 JFM MJJASOND/11 01320/1

Printed in Dongguan, Guangdong, China.

Contents

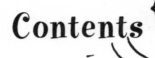

Chapter One   7

Chapter Two   17

Chapter Three   31

Chapter Four   45

Chapter Five   61

Chapter Six   72

Chapter
One

"Come one, come all! Who's going to have a try?" called a tall wizard in a crooked black hat. "Guess the number of eyeballs in the jar – win a cuddly vampire bat!"

"Dragon rides! Line up here for your dragon rides!" bellowed a red-haired giant, with an orange dragon flapping its leathery wings and puffing smoke behind him.

"Anyone for the Bouncy Dungeon?"
screeched a wart-nosed witch. "Only two
gold coins a turn!"

Oliver Moon stared around the Magic
School playing field, feeling shivery with
excitement. It was the school fair today,
and you could hardly see the grass for all

the stalls and sideshows that had been set up everywhere. Oliver was there with his family and his best friend, Jake Frogfreckle. He turned eagerly to Jake. "This looks fantastic!" he said. "What should we go on?"

Jake's eyes were shining happily. "Everything!" he replied.

Mr. and Mrs. Moon, Oliver's parents, chuckled at the looks on their faces. "Let's get some raffle tickets first," Mrs. Moon suggested, pushing the Witch Baby, Oliver's sister, along in her stroller toward a nearby stall. "There are some great prizes, look."

"Ooh, yes!" Jake said, elbowing Oliver as he read the sign. "Star prize — two tickets to see the Cacklewick Lightnings!"

Oliver's face lit up. The Cacklewick Lightnings was the local Wizardball team, and he and Jake were big fans. Unfortunately, tickets to their matches were really expensive and neither of the young wizards had ever been able to go and see a real game.

"This could be our lucky day, Jake,"

Oliver said excitedly. "Imagine if we won!"

Mrs. Moon took out her witch-wallet and paid for some raffle tickets. Then they set off for a good look around the fair.

First, Oliver and Jake tried out the Bouncy Dungeon, a huge inflatable room with real bats that flapped around you as you bounced. "Whoopee!" yelled Jake, arms flailing as he leaped up high.

"Whoa-a-a!" Oliver laughed, bouncing off the walls and feeling dizzy.

Then they went over to the Hook a
Frog stall, where they each managed
to catch a curious vanishing frog using
magic nets. "Well done, boys," the
stallholder said, giving them bags of
pet spiders as prizes.

Next, they tried the Lucky Dip, where
you had to plunge your hand into a
spooky dark cauldron and feel around for
a gift. Oliver pulled out a
color-changing pen, and
Jake got a glow-in-the-
dark badge in the
shape of a cat. And
then the Witch Baby
had a turn — and
leaned over so far, she fell
head first into the cauldron!

"Ooooh!" Oliver and Jake heard her cooing from inside. "Hello. Me win YOU!"

Mr. Moon hauled her out by her ankles to find her clutching a green toy imp. "Look!" she beamed. "He my prize!"

"Very nice," Mrs. Moon said, as the Witch Baby gave her prize a squelchy kiss.

Just then, the voice of Mrs. MacLizard, the head teacher, rang out across the field. She was standing on a stage, wearing a special gold cloak and a long purple dress. "Could everyone gather together over here, please? The raffle winners are about to be announced!"

Jake nudged Oliver excitedly. "Quick! Let's go and listen," he said. "Still feeling lucky?"

"You bet," Oliver said. "I'm telling you,

those Lightnings tickets are going to be ours, Jake. I've just got a feeling."

Oliver, his family and Jake made their way to the stage, along with lots of other witches and wizards. Mrs. MacLizard was holding a huge pointy hat with silver stars all over it, stuffed full of folded raffle ticket stubs.

Oliver's heart thumped as he held the ticket his mom had bought for him earlier. It was a shiny green color, with the number 279 written in swirly black numbers. "Come on, 279," he muttered under his breath, crossing his fingers. Oh, he *so* wanted to win those Wizardball tickets!

On stage, Mrs. MacLizard closed her eyes, delved a warty hand into the hat and pulled out a piece of paper. A magical drum roll filled the air as she opened it up, and Oliver held his breath.

"The first winning ticket is…number 279," Mrs. MacLizard announced. "Does anyone have number 279?"

Chapter Two

Oliver could hardly move, he was so stunned. Had he imagined that? Had Mrs. MacLizard really just said what he thought she'd said?

His mom was nudging him. "Oliver! That's your ticket. You've won!"

It was real! Suddenly Oliver's voice came back to him and he shouted out,

"Yes! Here!" and waved his ticket in the air.

Mrs. MacLizard smiled down at him. "Oliver Moon, you've won a lovely prize. Please come up onstage to receive it."

Oliver had never moved so fast in his whole life. *I knew it was my lucky day,* he thought to himself in a daze, as he rushed up the steps to the stage. *I just knew it!*

"Well done, Oliver," Mrs. MacLizard said. She was holding a large painting of the most hideous green monster Oliver had ever seen, with three eyes, six legs, two gigantic hands and a body that looked as if it were made of wobbly slime.

Ugh, Oliver thought, grimacing at the monster. Then he smiled up at his head teacher, waiting for her to give him his

prize. Oh yes. He could hardly wait to
hold those tickets!

Mrs. MacLizard didn't give him any
tickets though. She thrust the painting
into his arms instead. "There," she said
breezily. "Third prize. Something for your
bedroom wall, perhaps? Congratulations."

Oliver didn't move. Oh no! *This* was what he'd won?

"Ahh, look, everyone, he's overcome with happiness." Mrs. MacLizard smiled. "We'd like to thank the High Witch Arabella for donating such a...um...such a *unique* painting. A splendid prize!" She picked up the pointy hat and delved into it once more. "And the next winning number is..."

"Gutted," Jake said, shaking his head as Oliver came off the stage. "Thought you'd won the big prize for sure. They must be announcing that one at the end."

"Yeah." Oliver sighed. "And now I've got this horrible thing instead!" As he glumly put it down, the sun glinted off its gilt frame.

It seemed for a moment as if it were glittering extra-brightly, with hundreds of twinkles and sparkles shining all around, but then the sun slid behind a cloud and the sparkles disappeared.

His mom and dad inspected the painting curiously. "*Monster Mystery*, it's called," Mrs. Moon said, reading the label at the bottom of the frame.

"Yeah – it's a mystery why Arabella thought anyone would want to win that," Mr. Moon scoffed.

"Hmmm, well, it's not one I'd have chosen myself," Mrs. Moon said doubtfully. "But it's nice to win something, isn't it? And it's very kind of the High Witch Arabella to support our school…"

Mr. Moon snorted. "The High Witch Arabella is as nutty as a fruitcake," he said. "Always has been. Batty as a belfry. Barmy as a—"

"All right, not in front of the children," Mrs. Moon warned him in a low voice.

Oliver rolled his eyes at Jake. He wished the High Witch Arabella had kept her *Monster Mystery* to herself!

The raffle seemed to be drawing to a close. Oliver had been holding out a slim hope that Jake or even Mr. and Mrs. Moon would win the Lightnings tickets, but the last number called belonged to Arthur Silvertongue, one of the school monitors. Oliver couldn't help feeling a sickening twist of envy as Arthur went up onstage to collect the top prize and punched the air in triumph.

"Thank you, Mrs. MacLizard," he said happily, tucking the Lightnings tickets into his cloak pocket. "This is the best day of my life!"

The Moon family and Jake stocked up on snake cakes from the home-baked stall, then had a few turns on the Magic Helter-Skelter that whizzed you around at top speed. By now, the Witch Baby was drooping with tiredness in her stroller, so Oliver's parents decided it was time to head home.

They walked back, dropping Jake off at his house before going on to their own street. Once at home, Oliver tried out his new color-changing pen on a doodle pad and his sister played with her toy imp, while their parents made a pot of scrambled legs for dinner.

Before long, there was a shout of "Food's ready!" from the kitchen, and the Witch Baby toddled off, the imp tucked under her arm upside down. Oliver followed her in, and jumped slightly as he noticed that the monster painting had been hung up on the kitchen wall. He'd forgotten just how creepy the grinning green monster was!

"What do you think?" Mrs. Moon asked brightly, seeing his face. "Looks all right there, doesn't it? It's nice to have a splash of color in here."

"Um…" Oliver said. "I suppose so." He looked away hurriedly. There was something about the way the monster stared down at him that Oliver didn't like at all. He almost had the feeling that its mischievous eyes followed him around as he went to the table and sat down — very spooky!

Mr. Moon glanced over from where he was stirring some toenail sauce in a pitcher. "Hmmm," he said, stroking his chin thoughtfully as he saw where the painting had been hung. "I'm not so sure. I think it would be better over on the far wall. Let's see…" He pointed his wand at the painting.

"*Monster painting, hear my call,*
Hang yourself on this other wall!"
he chanted.

There was a flurry of bright purple sparks from Mr. Moon's wand and the painting glowed red for a second… but nothing else happened.

Mr. Moon frowned. "Strange," he said. He put the pitcher of sauce on the table then went over to the painting and tried to pull it off the wall. "How…peculiar!" Mr. Moon grunted, tugging at the painting with both hands. "It won't come away. It's stuck fast!"

It was true. No matter how hard Mr. Moon, Mrs. Moon or Oliver pulled

at the painting, it was firmly attached
to the wall, as if it were glued there.

"Great," Mr. Moon grumbled, when he
finally gave up. "Now we've got that
thing staring down at us for eternity!"

"I wonder if it's got some kind of old Sticking spell left on it?" Mrs. Moon said thoughtfully. "Oh well. We'll get used to it, I suppose. Give it a few days, and we'll barely notice that monster anymore."

The Moons picked up their silverware and started eating, but Oliver couldn't help glancing up at the painting again. He wasn't so sure his mom was right – it was such a horrible monster, he didn't think he'd *ever* get used to it being there!

Chapter Three

The next morning, Oliver woke to find his sister's face less than an inch from his. "Messy messy," she was saying urgently, shaking his pajama sleeve. "Ollie, come and see. Messy messy!"

"What's messy messy?" Oliver grumbled, shutting his eyes again and hoping she would go away.

But his sister merely pried his eyelids open with her stubby little fingers and repeated herself. "Messy! Come, Ollie!"

Oliver groaned and sat up. His sister's hair was wild and sticking up, and she had the toy imp tucked in her arms. Then she went and got Oliver's slippers and shoved them on the wrong feet. "There. Slip-slips on. You come now!"

"All right, all right," Oliver replied, rubbing his eyes. He'd been having such an exciting dream then as well, where he and Jake had gone to see the Cacklewick Lightnings beat their rivals, the Sludgeford Sluggers, eight—nothing.

He followed his sister downstairs, still yawning and wishing he could be back in bed. But as soon as he went into the kitchen, he forgot all about his dream and was jolted wide awake.

There was food *everywhere*! All of the cabinet doors had been flung open, with packages and cans knocked out onto the floor. There were broken bogey-cookies by the stove. Cat-whisker crackers lay scattered around the cauldron. And it looked as if a whole box of pig-tail pasta had been poured on the floor – in some kind of pattern…

"Messy *messy*," the Witch Baby said again in a solemn voice.

Oliver whistled. "Mom's going to flip her lid!" he said, running a hand through his hair. "Did you do this?"

The Witch Baby shook her head, wide-eyed. "Me NOT do it!" she replied.

"Well, then – who did?" Oliver wondered, shaking his head in horror. What a mess! Had they been robbed? Or…

He narrowed his eyes as he suddenly realized that the pig-tail pasta had been arranged very carefully, very deliberately, into the shape of letters. Words. There was a message in the pasta pattern!

Can…you…solve… he read, but before
he could make out any more, his sister
had blundered through the pasta, kicking
the pieces out of the way.

"Crunchy, crunchy," she chanted to
herself.

Oliver frowned, his mind still on the
pasta words. *Can you solve…*what?

Just then, his mom came in, tying the
belt of her robe. "Morning, kids,"
she said. "Did you sleep well?"

Then she clapped a
hand to her mouth
at the scene of chaos
and let out a scream.
"What's happened?"

"I don't know,"
Oliver said in a small
voice. "I didn't do it,
I didn't touch anything,
I just…"

Mrs. Moon was staring around the
room, her eyes looking as if they were
about to pop out of her head. "All this
food on the floor! What a state! A goblin
must have gotten in somehow, wretched
thing. I heard the Batbottoms had one
sniffing around the other day – it must
be the same one. What a pest!"

She waved her wand and muttered
a spell to return the cans and packages to
the cabinets, and then Oliver helped her
sweep up the spilled food. There even
seemed to be splotches of bright green
paint on the floor, which needed scrubbing
off. Where had that come from? Oliver's
mind was spinning, trying to make sense
of what had happened.

He wasn't so sure about his mom's explanation. A goblin getting into the kitchen and making a mess was one thing, but everyone knew that goblins couldn't even write their own names, let alone painstakingly spell out a message in pasta. Something weird was definitely going on – but what?

"There, that'll have to do," his mom said just then, tying a knot in the huge garbage bag. "Oliver, could you set the table for breakfast please, while I take this out to the trash can?"

"Sure," Oliver said, snapping out of his thoughts. He went toward the cabinet, where the Moons kept their silverware, bowls and plates, but before he got there a drawer slid open with a little wooden squeak. Oliver watched in amazement as a procession of knives, forks and spoons jumped up from inside the drawer and began prancing along in midair. Even the Witch Baby's pink plastic spoon was

there, bouncing merrily along behind the others, all the way to the kitchen table... where they plopped into the vase of wartweeds and glittered there, like strange silvery plants.

"What…? How…?" Oliver gulped, but something else was happening now. Four bowls and four plates floated up from their shelf and sailed through the air like magical boats, before landing on the table. Upside down. In a teetering tower!

Oliver rushed over at once, and was carefully unstacking the bowls and plates when his mom walked back in. "Oliver! What are you doing?" she cried.

Oliver jumped at the sound – and let go of the tower. CRASH! Down fell two bowls and a plate, smashing into jagged pieces on the stone floor.

"Oh, Oliver!" Mrs. Moon sighed,
getting out the dustpan and brush. "I've
just finished cleaning up the last mess in
here. And – oh! – what's the silverware
doing in that *vase*? Honestly!"

"But—" Oliver protested.

His mom didn't seem to want to listen.
"Go on – go upstairs and get dressed,"
she told him, running a hand through her

hair and looking cross. "I'm starting to wish I'd never gotten out of bed this morning!"

Oliver opened his mouth to argue, then shut it again. His mom looked so tired and fed up, she probably wouldn't believe him if he tried telling her that *he* hadn't stacked up the bowls and plates in a tower. Nor would she believe that he hadn't put the knives and forks in the vase. But it *hadn't* been him!

He traipsed upstairs, feeling confused. Why were so many peculiar things happening all of a sudden? It was a mystery. And if Oliver was going to get the blame for them, he definitely wanted some answers – and fast!

Chapter
Four

It was a good thing it was Sunday, as the
Moons ended up having a very late
breakfast that morning. "We're all going
out for the day," Mr. Moon said, when
Oliver came back downstairs after
getting dressed. He was sitting at the
table, munching on some batwing toast.
"It's perfect broomsticking weather, and

your mom's already made a picnic, so we can all fly off to Wilderness Woods as soon as we've eaten."

"Cool!" Oliver said, feeling more cheerful. Wilderness Woods was one of his favorite places. There were lots of huge dark trees that cast spooky shadows, and you could often spot beady-eyed rats weaving through the shrubbery.

Mrs. Moon was spooning Weevil-bix into the Witch Baby's mouth. "Yes, we've got bug-bread rolls, toad crisps, some slug cakes, cartons of worm juice…"

"Great," Oliver said, glancing up at the wicker picnic hamper that was sitting on the side. Then he blinked in shock. The lid of the hamper was opening and shutting very fast like

a big mouth. He rubbed his eyes and looked again. It was completely still now.

"Weird!" came a high-pitched voice just then, and Oliver turned in surprise.

"Who said that?" he asked, wondering if his dad was putting on a funny voice for a joke.

The Witch Baby's eyes were as bright as stars. She pointed at the toy imp that was tucked in her high chair alongside her. "Imp say it!" she spluttered through her cereal. "Imp TALK!"

The Moons all stared at the toy imp. Oliver jumped as its mouth suddenly opened. "Imps like playing tricks!" it said in the same high, squeaky voice.

Oliver's eyes bulged. "How is it doing that?" he marveled. He picked it up and looked at it closely. It was just an ordinary stuffed toy, with no buttons or switches anywhere. He shook it, then squeezed it, but nothing happened.

"There must be some kind of magic inside," Mrs. Moon said, eyeing it. "Very good value for a Lucky Dip toy, I must say."

"Imps like playing tricks," the imp said again in its naughty, high-pitched voice.

The Witch Baby beamed. "Me like twicks too," she replied, in a confiding way, patting it on the head.

Oliver stared suspiciously at the imp. Playing tricks, eh? Did that mean it could have been the *imp* who had made the mess in the kitchen, and magicked out the breakfast things? Surely that wasn't possible. Toys couldn't do things like that!

He thought hard. It did look as if there was some kind of magic in the imp, which had made it talk – and maybe had caused the other things to happen, too. Had the imp been enchanted by somebody, perhaps? But who? And why?

He finished his breakfast, unable to stop his mind from churning suspiciously. He would have to keep an eye on that imp! What was it going to do next?

A little later, the Moons went to get their cloaks and broomsticks, ready to set off to Wilderness Woods. Oliver's cloak rustled slightly as he put it on and he put

his hand into the
pocket, wondering
if he'd left a beetle-
bar wrapper or
something in there.
To his surprise, he
pulled out a folded
piece of paper with
his name on one
side in bright green
splotchy letters.
He unfolded it to
see some writing, the letters
shimmering all different colors as if the
words had been written with his new
color-changing pen. The message read:

Come on, Oliver, haven't you guessed?
Solve the mystery and pass the test!

He turned the paper over to see if there was any further message but the other side was blank. *Solve the mystery and pass the test?* What did that mean? What test?

"Ready? Let's go!" called his mom just then, and Oliver stuffed the note back into his cloak pocket and took off with the rest of his family as they soared up into the sky.

Once they got to Wilderness Woods, a wonderful time was had by all. First they went pond-dipping, and Oliver caught a lovely juicy water-snail which he gobbled up in a single bite. Then they fed the scrawny wild rats. "So cute! So cute!" the Witch Baby kept chirping each time one scampered up.

Then Oliver and his dad had a quick round of skull football. Perfect.

Oliver kept a close eye on his sister's imp the whole time. Any tricks from that creature and he'd spot them, he vowed!

So when Mr. and Mrs. Moon unpacked the picnic, Oliver watched the imp like a hawk, wondering if it might send the food flying somehow, or the drinks spilling...but nothing happened.

And when the Witch Baby got out her black bat-kite, Oliver suspected the imp might do something magical so that she became tangled in the string, but again...nothing happened.

The sun was starting to sink behind the trees when Mrs. Moon announced it was time to go home. "It's school tomorrow after all, and you've got some homework to finish, don't you, Oliver?" she reminded him.

Oliver sighed, thinking about his schoolwork. He had six potion recipes to learn, a page of Magical Math problems and a book on famous witches to read for the new class project. Ugh. Bor-ing! And of course, he hadn't done any of it yet.

Mr. Moon threw the last picnic crumbs to the rats, and Mrs. Moon gathered up their belongings. Then the four of them set off on their broomsticks for home again.

Back at the house, Oliver sat at the kitchen table and set out his books and pens. He leafed through his math book and found the first problem he had to solve.

Then his eyes widened as he saw what was printed there:

Mystery + magic + mischief = ?

He stared in surprise. That was a strange question. And there was a smear of green on the page too – just like the green splotches that had been on his weird note earlier. *And*, now he came to think about it, just like the green paint he'd found on the kitchen floor that morning. Where was it all coming from?

He frowned and flipped back a page in his math book to see the problems they'd been working on in class a few days earlier:

Three spider-legs + six fire-beetles (crushed)
= Twelve itching flakes
Nine owl hoots + a full moon +
two bat-wing flutters = Six rotten teeth
Four red toadstools + two yellow worm-heads
= Nine scarlet cheek-pimples

Those were *real* math problems — Oliver could do math like that. But this vague *Mystery + magic + mischief* business...

How was he supposed to answer that?

Oliver scratched his head – and then jumped as he noticed that one of his pens was rising up from the table all by itself. It turned gracefully in midair so that the nib pointed downward, then floated toward Oliver's open page and began to write in the space where the answer should go.

Hurry up, Oliver! the pen wrote.
Use your eyes!
When you find the answer,
you'll win a prize!

Oliver stared open-mouthed at the words and then gazed around the room, looking for his sister's toy imp. Had it caused this new magic? But the imp wasn't there.

He read the words again, trying to take them all in. Well, he'd won a prize yesterday and that hadn't done him much good, had it? He glanced up at the monster painting and jumped. The monster seemed to be grinning right at him again. In fact…

He blinked and stared harder. Had the monster in the picture just *winked* at him?

Chapter
Five

"Ooh!" Mrs. Moon exclaimed just then. "Was that lightning? Looks like a storm's on its way."

Oliver turned and looked out of the window where black thunderclouds were gathering in the sky. Then he smiled to himself. Imagine thinking a painting could wink! It must have been the flash of lightning that had made the monster's eyes flicker in that peculiar way.

He turned back to his math problems as the first fat drops of rain began spattering down outside. Thunder rumbled.

Right. Now to get on with this homework. *Mystery + magic + mischief.* Well…that could equal all kinds of trouble. In fact, the very sort of trouble he and his family had been experiencing — mysteriously spilled food, mischievously balanced plates and magically flying silverware! So… Oliver's eyes widened. This must be another clue!

"Mom!" he called. "Can you help me with something?"

Mrs. Moon had been chopping moldy

turnips for dinner, but at Oliver's words she put down the knife, wiped her hands on her apron and bustled over to him. "What is it?" she asked.

"Look what's written on my page," Oliver said, turning back to the book and pointing. Then he gaped. To his bewilderment, the *Mystery + magic + mischief* problem had vanished. So had the pen's magical message. In its place was a list of ordinary problems waiting to be completed.

"Number one: three shark eyes plus twelve minced crab claws equals…" Mrs. Moon read aloud. She wrinkled

her nose. "Ahh, I used to know this.
It's…um…twenty seagulls! Yes, seagulls.
Attracts them from all over." She looked
rather pleased with herself. "Imagine me
remembering that after all these years,"
she said, returning to her turnips.

"But—" Oliver started, flicking
through the pages of his book. He must

have turned one over by accident. Where was that magic writing? And that weird problem? It had totally disappeared!

"This is so strange," he muttered, feeling baffled. But it was getting late and he still had a stack of homework to get through. He didn't have time to ponder over it. He turned back to his problems and worked through them quickly, then picked up his book on famous witches. Mr. Goosepimple, Oliver's teacher, had asked the class to read chapter one: Great Witches Of Our Time.

"Fascinating stuff," Mr. Goosepimple had said. "The Witch Wars of 1710, the Great Witch Lucinda's rise to power and the tragedy of Drusilla the Mighty. Lots of action and drama! You can each choose one of the witches in this book to write a story about next week, so think about who you'd like to pick while you read."

Oliver turned to the first page, expecting to find the start of chapter one. To his surprise though, the writing at the top said *Chapter Six: Lesser-Known Witches*, with a picture underneath of a frizzy-haired woman with thick glasses, and a tall hat perched wonkily on her head.

Chapter six? thought Oliver. Where were the

first five chapters, then? Had the pages been printed in the wrong order?

He skimmed through quickly, searching for chapter one. But all he found was chapter six, again and again, with the same picture of the frizzy-haired witch staring shortsightedly at him. How weird! Then the caption underneath the picture caught his attention. It said: *The High Witch Arabella de Nightshade, best known for her mischievous sense of humor and practical jokes.*

The High Witch Arabella? She was the one who'd donated the monster picture to the Magic School Fair! But wait... *Best known for her mischievous sense of humor and practical jokes*? Did that mean...could that mean that *Arabella* had something to do with all the strange happenings in the Moon house?

The words from the book raced through his mind. Ever since he'd won the monster painting, there had been an awful lot of weird things happening — it *was* exactly as if practical jokes were being played on the family.

Then something else clicked in his brain. Hadn't his mom said back at the fair that the monster painting was called *Monster Mystery*?

He turned and stared at the green monster in the painting. And then he noticed that there was a scattering of pasta pieces around the monster's feet and a pen in one of its hands.

"It's you!" he cried, realizing that the

green painty splot es he'd seen lately were the exact same green as the monster. Somehow it must have been clambering out of its painting! "It's you, isn't it, who's been playing tricks?"

At Oliver's words, the painting suddenly flashed different colors...and the monster in the picture licked its lips in a hungry sort of way.

Monster Mystery

"It's alive!" Oliver cried. Even though he'd realized the truth, it was still a shock to see the picture moving like that.

"Mom – the painting's alive!"

And right as he said those words, the monster's arm shot straight out of the painting – and grabbed Oliver!

Mrs. Moon screamed and dropped her chopping knife with a clatter. "Get off him!" she yelled at the monster.

Mr. Moon raced in. "What's going on?" he shouted.

Everything happened very quickly then. The monster's whole body came out of the painting and jumped down into the kitchen, still holding Oliver with one of its giant hands. Then, before Oliver could move, the monster had scooped him up under one massive arm, grabbed the painting – now empty of any picture – and had run right out of the house.

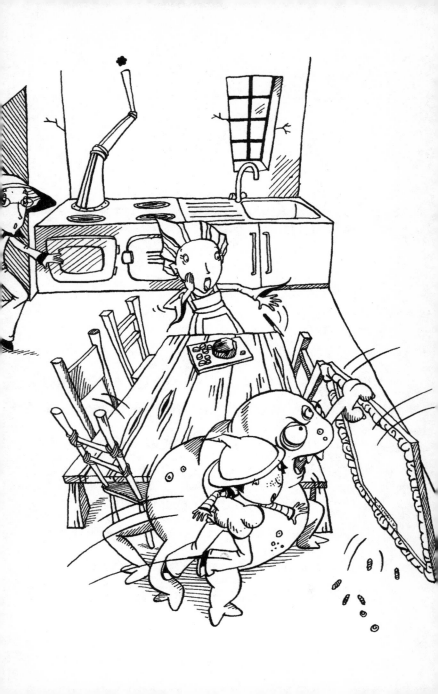

Chapter Six

Oliver was terrified. He had no idea where the monster was taking him, or what was going to happen next. "Put me down!" he yelled. "I want to go home!"

But the monster didn't listen. Over its shoulder, Oliver could see that his parents had run out of the house and were chasing after them through the thunderstorm.

"Bring him back!" Mrs. Moon screeched.

"Hold on, Oliver!" Mr. Moon called. "I'll get my broomstick. I'll fly after you! I..."

His voice grew fainter and fainter as
the monster galloped further away,
scarily fast. Oliver couldn't hear his
parents anymore. They were specks in the
distance. And now the monster was

running through creepy
Cacklewick Forest,
which was said to be
full of poisonous
snakes and attack-bats
that lurked in the
treetops.

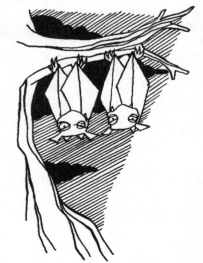

"Where are we
going?" he asked,
his voice wobbling
with fear. The
trees were dripping
with water as rain

streamed through their leaves, and thunder was rumbling ominously in the background. Oh, how Oliver wished he'd never won the monster painting in the first place!

After a few minutes, the monster stopped dead in front of a ramshackle old cottage deep in the forest. Oliver's heart thudded painfully as he peered through the pouring rain. Now what? Was this where the monster lived?

The monster, still carrying Oliver, lumbered up the path that led to the front door. Nettles and venom-shrubs grew wild in the garden, and Oliver could see yellow eyes peering at him from the undergrowth, where hidden creatures sheltered from the storm.

The door of the cottage swung open as the monster approached, and a witch appeared in the doorway. She had wild frizzy hair, thick glasses, and wore a red dress that clashed horribly with her

green and pink striped tights. She also had a black purring cat draped around her shoulders, which opened one green eye to peer curiously at Oliver.

Oliver's mouth went dry as he recognized her. He licked his lips. It was the High Witch Arabella, he was sure of it! But what was she going to do? Why had the monster brought him to her?

The witch clapped her hands, looking delighted. "Come in, Igor, there's a good boy," she said to the monster, holding the door wide for him.

The monster obediently went through the front door, and set Oliver down on the floor, along with the picture frame. But as they entered the cottage, something amazing happened. The walls shone gold – such a bright gold that Oliver had to shield his eyes from the dazzling glare. When he uncovered them, the monster had vanished completely.

Oh! No, he hadn't! He was back in the painting, waving and grinning. And Oliver wasn't standing in a rundown old  cottage as he'd expected. The room he was in seemed fit to belong in a palace, with its high vaulted ceilings, studded with sparkling jewels. The walls were white-gold, with stained-glass windows shining all colors as the sun streamed in through them. A cauldron bubbled merrily in the white-brick hearth, and a dozen or so cats were curled up on a rug in front of it.

"But…" Oliver started, gazing around in confusion. "But…?"

"Surprised?" the witch cackled, seeing Oliver's face. "My little trick. I make the outside of this place look shabby to keep the robbers away. Good, eh?" She cackled again, a friendly, cheerful sort of a noise, which made Oliver feel slightly less scared all of a sudden.

"I don't understand," he said shyly. "Why am I here?"

"Allow me to introduce myself," the witch said, smiling at him. "My name is the High Witch Arabella, as I think you guessed. And you must be the clever little wizard who solved my monster mystery. Welcome!"

Oliver was still trying to make sense of

everything. "So you gave the painting to the school raffle…" he said slowly.

"That's right," Arabella replied. "But it wasn't an ordinary painting, was it? I thought it would be more fun if there was a mystery to solve. So I put a good dollop of mischief magic into the paint. Have lots of funny things been happening to you since you won the painting?"

Oliver nodded. "Yes," he said.

Arabella looked very pleased to hear it. "Excellent!" she cackled. "I like to keep things interesting!" She grinned at Oliver. "So now that you've solved my puzzle and realized my little monster was behind everything, you'd better have your real prize."

"My real prize?" Oliver echoed.

"Oh yes," Arabella said. "Of course!" She waved her wand, and a shining ball of golden vapor landed gently on Oliver's hand. "It's a wish," she told him. "You can wish for anything you like."

Oliver felt a rush of excitement. He knew just what he was going to wish for! "I wish I had..." Then he paused to count. Him, Jake, Mom, Dad, his sister... "Five tickets to see the Cacklewick Lightnings next Saturday, please!" he said.

The golden vapor evaporated with a little puffing sound, and Oliver let out a cheer as five tickets to the match appeared in his hand. "Thank you, thank you!" he cried. "That's the best prize ever!"

Arabella smiled. "Oh good," she said. "So glad you like it. And now I'd better whisk you off home. I sent a magic message to your parents telling them not to worry as soon as I heard that Igor was on his way – but I guess they'd like to see you safe and sound again."

"Thank you," Oliver said once more, throwing his arms around her on impulse, and nearly knocking the black cat from its perch. He still couldn't believe he'd gotten a set of Lightnings tickets. Talk about a happy ending!

Arabella tapped her wand on his head, and the world seemed to spin around very fast. Everything blurred before Oliver's eyes and he just had time to shout out a quick goodbye before he felt his feet lift off the ground. Then he seemed to be traveling at a great speed, faster and faster, hurtling through bright white light…

Bump! Down he landed in his very own kitchen — and there were his mom, dad and sister, all looking at him with astonished faces.

"You're back!" Mrs. Moon cried, hugging him. "Have you really been to the High Witch Arabella's house?"

"Yes," Oliver managed to get out through his mom's tight squeeze.

Mr. Moon hugged Oliver too. "I told you Arabella was bonkers. Didn't I tell you?"

"I like her," Oliver said, smiling. "That was the best prize ever — having the monster mystery to solve! And that's not the only thing. Look what Arabella gave me!" He held out his hand, showing the Wizardball tickets, and his family gathered around to see.

"Oooh, fantastic!" his mom squealed excitedly.

His dad looked delighted too. "I take it all back about Arabella," he declared. "Always thought she was a wonderful witch. Isn't that what I said? One of the best!"

Oliver gazed happily at the tickets. He couldn't wait to tell Jake the great news — and he couldn't wait for the match itself. He was even looking forward to going back to school tomorrow and starting the new class project on famous witches. He had a feeling *his* story would be a very exciting one indeed!

The End

Don't miss Oliver's fab website,
where you can find lots of fun, free stuff.
Log on now...

www.olivermoon.com

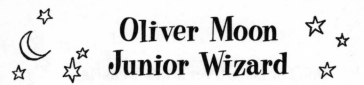

Oliver Moon
Junior Wizard

Collect all of Oliver Moon's magical adventures!

Oliver Moon and the Potion Commotion
Can Oliver create a potion to win the Young Wizard of the Year award?

Oliver Moon and the Dragon Disaster
Oliver's sure his new pet dragon will liven up the Festival of Magic...

Oliver Moon and the Nipperbat Nightmare
Things go horribly wrong when Oliver gets to look after the school pet.

Oliver Moon's Summer Howliday
Oliver suspects there is something odd about his hairy new friend, Wilf.

Oliver Moon's Christmas Cracker
Can a special present save Oliver's Christmas at horrible Aunt Wart's?

Oliver Moon and the Spell-off
Oliver must win a spell-off against clever Casper to avoid a scary forfeit.

Oliver Moon's Fangtastic Sleepover
Will Oliver survive a school sleepover in the haunted house museum?

Oliver Moon and the Broomstick Battle
Can Oliver beat Bully to win the Junior Wizards' Obstacle Race?

Happy Birthday, Oliver Moon
Will Oliver's birthday party be ruined when his invitations go astray?

Oliver Moon and the Spider Spell
Oliver's Grow-bigger spell lands the Witch Baby's pet in huge trouble.

Oliver Moon and the Troll Trouble
Can Oliver save the show as the scary, stinky troll in the school play?

Oliver Moon and the Monster Mystery
Strange things start to happen when Oliver wins a monster raffle prize...